Summer Lovin':
Wet Dreams
Come True

Alexa Ambrose

ISBN: 9781793315229

DEDICATION

For the girls, because you believed.

CONTENTS

ACKNOWLEDGMENTS

Alexa would like to thank her husband and family for their support during the writing and development of her first story. She is also forever grateful to her besties for their belief in her abilities to write and self-publish her stories, their encouragement and availability at weird and wonderful times for a glass of wine!

1 SUMMER HEAT

It had been a long, hot summer and Imogen was feeling restless. She wished that the heat would simmer down to a mild, temperate degree that would buoy her spirits and motivate her to work through her To Do List. Instead, it was sweltering hot and Imogen's only relief was the cool, crystal waters of her swimming pool.

It was so blissful, just to dive in and feel all the sticky heat sluicing off her, leaving her feeling naked and reborn. Lap after lap, Imogen glided through the water feeling the ripples of water caress her smooth skin. Once she finally felt she'd reached a pleasant equilibrium, Imogen emerged from the water and lay on her sun lounge to dry off.

As the heat warmed her cool skin Imogen closed her eyes and let her fingers softly trace swirls across the skin of her stomach, breasts and hips as the water beaded and evaporated from her skin.

Austin watched as Imogen's fingers feathered over her body from his concealed position in the upper bedroom window. He mirrored her movements as he stroked the length of his erect cock. Austin had first seen Imogen out by the pool a couple of weeks ago, and having fantasized about his beautiful, young step-mother since he'd first reached puberty it had been like a gift from the gods to look out the window one summer day and see the object of his deepest fantasies lying in the sun, gently caressing herself.

Austin's cock jerked against his strong, rough hand as Imogen's slender fingers swirled up over her breasts, traced circles around her cherry sized nipples and then with her thumb and index finger gave them a soft, rolling twist that caused them to pucker and harden before returning to the feathering movements over her torso.

Austin imagined that it was Imogen's hands stroking his hardness as he increased the pressure of his movements. His balls tightened as she arched her back whilst fondling and squeezing her delectable breasts. Austin pictured Imogen arching up as he took her ripe cherry nipples into his mouth, suckling and gently grazing them with his teeth. He could almost taste her musky sweetness as he moved his own hand rhythmically over his swollen and aching cock. Pearls of pre-cum glistened and Austin swirled the pre-cum over the head of his cock with his thumb just as Imogen had done with her nipples. It was exquisite torture to watch Imogen, to imagine himself doing those things to her just as he had dreamed for years.

Years of yearning and desire mingled, building into a crescendo. Hot, thick semen spurted from Austin's cock, marring the view of Imogen through the window. Austin thrust and milked every last drop as he dreamed of one day blowing his load all over Imogen for real.

As pleasurable as it was, Imogen had had enough playing. There were other things to do. As she opened her eyes Imogen caught a glimpse of Austin in the upstairs window, cock in hand. She blinked and looked again, but the window was empty. Had she imagined it? The thought of her barely legal step-son watching her should have shocked and repulsed her, but Imogen was strangely turned on.

In fact, Imogen hadn't felt this turned on in years. Her husband had been focused only on achieving his own pleasure once the honeymoon had ended and she'd preferred to service her own needs than have her much older husband heave himself on top of her, grunting and gasping for breath. It hadn't occurred to her until now that little Austin was all grown up - no longer little, but now a man, with manly needs. A younger, more virile version of her aging husband, ripe for the picking and eager to learn? Perhaps Imogen could teach him how to satisfy a woman. It was perfect. Suddenly everything on Imogen's To Do List evaporated, fading into obscurity in the light of her new goal.

Austin nearly had a heart attack when he saw Imogen open her eyes and look straight up at his window. He'd quickly backed out of sight - so much for concealed position! How was he ever going to look his step-mother in the eye again? It was one thing to secretly have your step-mother in your spank bank, it was another thing altogether for her to see you yanking your own chain.

There was a knock at his bedroom door and Austin's heart sank. This was it. The woman who had been like a second mother to him was going to give him a blistering earful, and threaten to tell his father what a dirty little pervert he was. It was humiliating. Austin resigned himself to the inevitable and went to open it. As he'd expected, he found Imogen waiting.

"Austin?"

"Hey Imogen, what can I do for you today?" Austin tried to play it cool.

"If you're not busy, I was hoping you could help me out with something?"

"Um, sure. I'll be right out." Austin was confused but relieved; perhaps Imogen hadn't see anything after all.

2 THE OFFER OF A LIFETIME

"Just this way," said Imogen as she led Austin down the hall. Austin followed along, wondering what Imogen wanted his help with. Imogen opened the door that led into the suite of rooms she shared with his father and turned to face Austin. "I saw you earlier."

"Uh-" Austin wasn't sure what to say.

Imogen sat down on a chaise and gestured for Austin to take a seat. "It's ok, you're not in trouble. I'm just curious - were you watching me for long?"

Austin figured there was nothing to be gained by lying, so he admitted that he'd been watching her since she'd been doing laps.

"And is this the first time you've watched me?" she asked playfully, expecting him to tell her it was the first time he'd ever done anything like this.

"Er.. Not exactly." Austin took a deep breath, "The first time I saw you, um, at the pool, was a couple of weeks ago."

Imogen was stunned. He'd been watching her for weeks, and she'd only just noticed! Clearly she needed to be a little more aware of her surroundings. Her heart rate sped up as she grasped the implications of what he'd just confessed. Austin had been watching her for weeks. Watching her caress and fondle herself by the pool, presumably whilst playing along, for *weeks*. He actually *fantasized* about her. For all that she'd planned to seduce him once she'd realized he'd seen her earlier that day, it hadn't occurred to her that this was an ongoing attraction on his part.

Imogen could feel the slick moisture building in her core. It was such an erotic thrill to be the object of someone's fantasy - no one had ever made her feel this way before. Certainly not her husband, who fantasized more about football than he did about her.

Imogen was simultaneously struck by a sadness that she'd wasted so much time with someone who had made her feel less than adequate. She realized that while she'd thought that servicing her own needs was enough, all she'd really done was reinforce those feelings of inadequacy. She'd never given herself, or anyone else the opportunity to embrace her inner goddess, to help her blossom sexually. It had taken her husband's son to make her see that.

Imogen was determined not to let this opportunity pass her by. She deserved this, she needed Austin. Imogen knew she was going to have to step out of her comfort zone and take charge.

❧

While all these thoughts tumbled through Imogen's mind, Austin sat there fearing the worst. Now that he'd confessed the whole, dirty secret surely Imogen would be furious at him for his perversion. He started to apologize, to promise her that he'd never do it again when Imogen cut him off- "Do you think I'm sexy, Austin?"

"Y-yes, Imogen." Austin stuttered, hardly knowing where this was leading.

"Do you want to fuck me?"

Austin couldn't believe his ears. "Sorry, what did you just say?"

"Let's cut to the chase, Austin. I've come to the realization that I need a real man to satisfy my needs, and here you've been fantasizing about fucking me. Seems we could come to an accommodation, don't you agree?"

Never in his wildest dreams had Austin imagined that he would hear these words come out of Imogen's mouth. He'd been fantasizing about his hot step-mother for so long, and now his fantasies were about to become reality. His cock had hardened as Imogen had spelled things out for him, and he was practically creaming himself at the thought of thrusting his cock into Imogen's hot, wet pussy, pounding her incessantly until she screamed.

❈

Imogen took note as Austin's cock strained against his trousers. Clearly he was receptive to her deal. A sudden thought occurred to her, "Austin, before we get carried away - have you been tested recently?"

Austin looked at her blankly. "Tested?"

"For sexually transmitted diseases. When was the last time you were tested?"

Austin blushed and mumbled, "I've never been tested. I... I'm a virgin."

Imogen's jaw dropped, "Seriously? Austin, you're tall, handsome, popular... every girl's dream - how is it that you're still a virgin?"

"You know Dad. He's always made such a big deal about how I should wait until I met the girl of my dreams. That sex brings responsibilities, and if I wasn't prepared to do "the right thing" then I had no business pushing myself on some poor girl. Somewhere along the way I guess it just felt like the right thing to do. And, if I needed company in the meantime, he said I could give myself a hand."

"Oh." Imogen was at a loss for words; she could hear her husband's words echoing in her head. She should have known better; her husband was all about 'responsibility' and 'obligation'. Clearly Austin was not going to be tempted by her offer after all.

"But-" Austin went on, "You're the only woman I've ever dreamed about. I just never thought it was a possibility with you being married to my Dad and all, but I could never settle for less. I'm all in, Imogen. It's only ever been you."

Imogen was speechless and incredibly aroused. Just when she thought Austin couldn't get any more perfect, somehow he did. This young, virginal Adonis had been fantasizing about and saving himself *for her*. Imogen sent a silent prayer of thanks to her husband for raising his son to be so 'responsible'. Years of unexpressed bitterness and resentment melted away at the thought of her step-son vigorously filling his father's shoes.

Taking Austin by the hand, Imogen led him further into the bedroom. The carved wooden four poster bed she shared with Austin's father stood in the center of the room.

Neatly made with crisp pale wheat colored sheets and a matching cream and gold coverlet, the bed looked serene, sophisticated and inviting. Imogen shrugged off the caftan she'd slipped on before knocking on Austin's door, and turned to face him, clad only in her scant bikini. Austin hesitantly removed his shirt, revealing his well-formed chest and chiseled abs. He started to unbutton his trousers when Imogen stepped forward to assist him.

Imogen stepped close enough that her lush breasts brushed against Austin's chest as she slowly slipped her hands to the button of his trousers. She popped the button open and drew down the zipper, following its descent with her body until she'd sunk to her knees, her wide mouth level with Austin's straining manhood.

Imogen ran her hands sensuously up Austin's muscular thighs, hooked the waistband of his briefs in her fingertips and slowly, teasingly drew them down until his thick cock burst forth, finally released from its confinement. A magnificent specimen - so different from his father's limp whistle - it stood boldly at attention, flexing against Austin's abdomen. Imogen ran her tongue lightly up the length of his staff, taking the engorged head into her warm, wet mouth and applying gentle pressure along the tip with her teeth.

Austin shuddered with pleasure and reached for Imogen, twining her silky hair in his fists and pushing himself deeper into her mouth. She sucked and swirled her tongue over his steely hard rod while bringing her right hand around to cup his balls in her palm. She gently squeezed and rolled his testes in her hand as she sucked and felt him stiffen even harder.

Lost in the exquisite pleasure of her ministrations, it was all Austin could do not to come then and there. Much as he desperately wanted to blow his load into Imogen's sweet mouth and watch her swallow his seed, he needed to regain control and show Imogen that while he might be a virgin, he was not an inexperienced little boy. He was a man, and he wanted to pleasure her as much, and more than she had ever been pleasured before.

Austin used his grasp on her hair to carefully disengage her from his throbbing cock and urge Imogen back into a standing position where he pulled her into a raw, searing kiss. He tasted the saltiness of himself on her lips, feeling a primal, possessive urge within him triumph.

Imogen had never been kissed with such earthy intensity. As Austin took possession of her mouth she could feel his mighty erection pressing against her, sending jolts of pure electricity straight to her own groin. She hooked one of her legs around his and pulled him closer as she sank deeper into the kiss. Imogen could feel the slick wetness seeping between her legs, her inner walls throbbing with need.

Austin untangled his fingers from Imogen's silky hair and trailed his hands down her back to cup her firm, pert buttocks. He pulled her up hard against him, pressing his pulsating erection against the thin veil of her bikini briefs. Austin subtly squeezed and softened his grasp on her buttocks so that his erection grazed up and down her cleft, teasing the hot button of her desire. Imogen moaned with unrestrained need, wondering how this virginal god could know just what it was that pressed her buttons.

With one last thrust against her cleft, Austin pushed Imogen down onto the bed and lowered his head to nibble a trail of sensuous kisses down her neck. He untied the strings of her bikini top as his mouth worked its way down, releasing her round, soft breasts.

Cupping her gorgeous tits together with his strong hands, he finally paid the homage to the luscious cherry sized nipples that he'd dreamed of earlier. As in his fantasy, Imogen arched her back, thrusting her perfect breasts closer, urging him to take her taut nipples into his mouth. He tasted her musky sweetness, suckling one nipple while rolling the other nipple between his thumb and forefinger as he'd seen Imogen do to herself.

Imogen felt the desire pulse straight from her tender, electrified nipples deep into her sex, the heat of her longing threatening to shatter her like glass. With one hand occupied with teasing her nipple, Austin slipped his other hand beneath the elastic of her bikini briefs and trailed a finger along her slick, wet folds. It gave him a thrill to know that he had made this goddess of his fantasies so wet and horny for him.

❧

With both hands, Austin slipped off Imogen's bikini briefs, baring her sex to him fully. He had never seen anything so perfect. He ran his hands purposefully up her creamy thighs, spreading them wide as he reached the apex of her womanhood. Using his fingers to prise apart her slick, wet folds, Austin took stock of Imogen's swollen clit, wondering at the epicenter of her desire.

Once again, he lowered his head, this time to taste her sweet pussy nectar. Oh how Austin had dreamed of this moment. He laved her seam with his tongue, lapping at her aching clitoris until she cried out in shivering delight. Imogen squirmed and bucked as Austin's skillful tongue drove her wild. She nearly came apart as he slid two of his large fingers into her throbbing pussy while continuing his assault on her vulva. As he slowly thrust his fingers in and out, Imogen felt the slow burn inside her building into a raging inferno.

Austin continued to nip at her sensitive bud of desire whilst rhythmically moving his fingers in and out of her slit, increasing the pressure at irregular intervals that made her desire spiral to dizzying heights. With his free hand, Austin took one of her still sensitized cherry nipples between his thumb and forefinger and started to roll and twist it the way Imogen loved, puckering and peaking the sensitive tip.

It was all too much for Imogen; the combined assault on her nipples, her throbbing clitoris and the delicious thrusting of his fingers in her pussy brought her to a loud, screaming climax. Imogen saw stars as Austin fucked her pussy hard with his fingers, stretching and filling her. "Oh Austin, Fuck me now! I need to feel that rock hard cock of yours inside me!" she begged. "Please!"

Austin didn't need any further encouragement. His balls were so tight and his cock was aching to be inside her. Now that he'd brought her to climax he wasted no time replacing his fingers with his cock, the aftershocks of her orgasm clenching her walls tight around him. He groaned with pleasure as he pounded into her, the head of his cock slamming up against her cervix over and over.

Imogen splayed her hands over Austin's chest as he fucked her, teasing his nipples as he had done hers. His nipples puckered and tightened and he shuddered at the exquisiteness of feeling. Austin lifted one of Imogen's legs over his shoulder, penetrating deeper and deeper into her core. Imogen could feel the pleasure building inside her again with the constant friction of his thrusts. Her husband had never fucked her like this. He'd never thrust so deep into her, never filled her so completely with his manhood. Funny that it should be his own virgin son who would teach her so much about pleasure.

As Austin continued to ram into her with his unrelenting cock, the velvety head grazed against Imogen's sensitive G-spot. "Oh yes! Fuck me harder!" she screamed. Austin lifted Imogen's other leg over his shoulder and pressed his steely rod deeper into her. Imogen nearly levitated off the bed as his cock butted up against her G-spot and triggered a tidal wave of pleasure that radiated through Imogen's entire body. Imogen screamed and cried out as the intensity of her orgasm shook her, in an unparalleled feeling of pure, bone deep gratification.

Austin groaned as the full force of her orgasm clenched his cock in rolling waves of pleasure. He couldn't hold on any longer, her spasming pussy begging to be filled with his hot, sticky seed. Austin thrust as hard and fast as he could, giving himself over to the primal need to dominate by battering the soft flesh of her cervix with his hardness. As Imogen's pussy clenched and pulsed, Austin's climax crashed over him like a wave. He filled her full of his thick cum, spurting it high within her as he milked his aching balls dry.

Imogen felt exulted as his potent essence gushed deep inside, drowning her pussy and filling every crevice. As Austin slowly withdrew and lay next to her, Imogen felt boneless and satiated in a way she'd never experienced before.

3 SWEET RELEASE

As they both came down from their endorphin rush, Imogen turned to Austin with a slow, sweet smile. "And you say you've never done this before? My God, you were amazing!"

Austin drew her close and whispered, "Just think how much better I'll be with practice!"

Imogen could feel his staff already at attention again, and thanked the gods for youthful enthusiasm and stamina. "Mmm, indeed," she purred, "Practice makes perfect." Imogen tilted up to give him a soft, lingering kiss, pressing her body against his.

❈

Austin levered Imogen onto her back, rising above her and nudging her thighs apart. Her pussy was slick with their mingled juices as Austin reached down to cup her mound in his hand. His fingers parted her nether lips to expose her tender nub, softly teasing it with his thumb. As his thumb circled, he slipped two fingers into her pussy, pressing deep and high, causing Imogen to moan and push her peachy softness up into his palm.

Austin brought his hand up to Imogen's lips, his fingers coated in their glistening juices. Imogen locked her eyes with Austin's as she parted her lips, allowing him to penetrate her mouth with his fingers. Imogen licked and sucked their combined fluid from them, marveling in the sweet, salty earthiness of their sap. Austin watched as she lapped at his fingers, sucking up and swallowing every bit of his sticky cum and her own pussy nectar. He removed his fingers and leaned down to taste their pleasure from her lips. As their tongues entwined, the flavor of their lovemaking enveloped them, burnishing their mutual need.

Austin's cock flexed in response, brushing against Imogen's creamy thigh. She reached for his rod, taking it firmly in her hand and gently squeezed it once, then twice, stroking as she guided it back to the entrance of her vulva. Imogen wrapped her legs around Austin's waist as she enticed him to enter her. Austin deepened the kiss as he pressed forward; his staff delving deep into her slippery sheath. Imogen squeezed her legs together as Austin moved rhythmically in and out, urging him deeper.

Suddenly, Austin pulled out, and Imogen whimpered at the sudden emptiness. He flipped Imogen onto her hands and knees, bringing her sweet, round ass high against him. Austin positioned his tumescent cock at the entrance to her pussy and with small, sensuous rocking movements back and forth, dipped the swollen head of his cock in and out of her quivering cunt making her cry out with need.

For Austin, the sensation of entering her just enough to envelop the highly sensitized head of his cock before pulling out and entering again was maddeningly erotic. Finally Austin couldn't bear to tease himself any longer and plunged fully into Imogen, his hands grasping her hips and pulling her sweet rear up to meet his every thrust.

Imogen spread her knees further apart so she could feel him pounding deep inside her. Her clit ached with longing so she reached between her legs to stroke and kindle the fire again. As Austin hammered her inner walls, Imogen dipped her slender fingers into her wet, slippery seam, swirling and coaxing her clit to attention. Austin loved that he was fucking her from behind, thrusting his engorged cock into her pussy while Imogen's fingers worked her clitoris into a fevered frenzy. There was something so illicitly sexual about fucking a woman as she masturbated.

Austin felt her sheath tighten around him and reached forwards to fondle and squeeze her full breasts. Imogen moaned as Austin massaged her breasts, his ministrations causing her nipples to pucker as he thrummed over them purposefully with his thumbs. As her nipples peaked, Austin pinched them both firmly between his fingers and twisted gently, his fingers weaving their sensual magic until Imogen was sobbing with pleasure.

Imogen was overwhelmed with raw sensation, her tight, swollen nub blossoming as her fingers moved in concert with Austin's powerful thrusts. Imogen keened as she found sweet, mind-blowing release, crying out for Austin to fuck her hard. Austin felt Imogen's pussy seize him and reveled in the sensation of her orgasmic embrace. As her walls convulsed and clenched around him, Austin slammed his rod harder into her cunt, burying himself to he hilt.

With each powerful thrust, Austin penetrated Imogen deeper, seeking his own fulfillment as he sought to impale her. As Austin dominated Imogen's sweet pussy his own climax surged into a potent flood-tide, his seed gushing forth in a powerful jet-stream. Austin groaned as his cock continued to erupt, pulsing and heaving his hot semen into her eager passage. His load spent, Austin collapsed down to lay next to Imogen, their vigorous lovemaking having exhausted his youthful power reserves.

Imogen lay replete in a sensuous languor; her body tingling and spread with a pleasurable warmth. As Austin recharged and relaxed by her side, Imogen thanked her lucky stars for the long, hot summer. Had she not felt so unpleasantly hot and sticky earlier, she'd never have gone swimming, which in turn wouldn't have led to her current pleasantly warm and sticky state.

In her wildest dreams, Imogen would never have imagined that her husband's son could be the answer to all her most erotic fantasies. She looked forward to exploring those fantasies with Austin - but first, it was time for another swim.

Stay tuned for Alexa's next book, continue on for a hot
sneak peek…

EXCERPT – SUMMER FANTASY

I was about to turn back to the party when I noticed a derelict boathouse up ahead. As I carefully made my way towards the boathouse I heard a noise, like a woman's muffled scream. I took a deep breath, steadying myself as I wavered in my desire to flee back to the party. What if someone was in trouble? How could I just walk away?

I turned off the light on my phone as I crept closer to the boathouse. As I reached the battered doors: old, rotted and barely holding to the hinges, I heard the sound of something striking bare flesh.

"That's right! I saw you! Fawning all over that asshole like he was a God. Letting him put his hands on you. You fucking horny bitch!"

I gasped as I recognized Ethan's voice, his words so out of character for the person I knew. The mystery woman moaned in response, and I heard the sound of struck flesh again.

"You want hands on you? I'll lay my hands on you!" Ethan growled.

I'd heard enough, this couldn't possibly be the Ethan that I knew; the Ethan that I'd been fantasizing about for years. I must be mistaken. Either way, I couldn't stand by and him treat the mystery girl that way; it just wasn't right.

I slipped through the rotted doors, trying carefully not to brush against them lest the hinges finally give way and create a racket. It took a moment for my eyes to adjust to the darkness inside the boathouse; finally I was able to make out shapes of objects illuminated by slivers of moonlight that peeked through the decaying boards that made up the walls. As my eyes adjusted further, I heard grunting and made my way carefully towards the sound. I rounded a rack of boating equipment and stopped dead in my tracks. Nothing I'd imagined could have prepared me for the scene in front of me.

Moonlight shone through high, wide glass windows built into the upper walls of the boathouse on the lake side, the silvery light bouncing and reflecting off the still water in the mooring bay and softly illuminating the interior of the boathouse. From my position near the storage racks, I could see the mystery girl, clad only in her bikini top, on all fours, bent over a set of wooden steps as a magnificently naked Ethan stood behind her and slammed his hips towards her rear, using his strong, firm hands to grip her hips and pull her to meet his thrusts. He raised one hand and brought it down in a stinging slap as he continued to thrust towards the girl who moaned… in pleasure.

ABOUT THE AUTHOR

Alexa Ambrose unashamedly loves a good Disney movie, and is a sucker for those sweet happily ever after endings. *Summer Lovin'* is her debut erotic story, originally published as a Kindle ebook in 2015. After a hiatus to travel the world and spend time exploring Italy, Alexa looks forward to the release of her second story *Summer Fantasy* in September 2019.

You can find Alexa on Twitter @IamAlexaAmbrose